The New Roof

by Emma DeBrose
illustrated by Joy Allen

Fixit Family Series

The New Roof
Author: Emma DeBrose

Heinemann
361 Hanover Street
Portsmouth, NH 03801–3912
www.heinemann.com

Offices and agents throughout the world

Fountas and Pinnell Leveled Literacy Intervention Books
Copyright © 2009 by Irene C. Fountas, Gay Su Pinnell, and Heinemann

ISBN-13: 978-0-325-02017-4   ISBN-10: 0-325-02017-5

Editorial Development, Design, and Production by Brown Publishing Network

Credits
Illustrations: Joy Allen

Printed in China
10 11 12 13 14 15 16 RRD 8 7 6 5

The New Roof

by Emma DeBrose
illustrated by Joy Allen

Nana   Pop   Mom   Matt   Rose

The Fixit family lived
in an old house.
It had old walls
and old windows
and an old, old roof.

"We have to fix that roof,"
Nana said.
"It's going to rain soon."

3

"I can fix it," said Pop.

"I can fix it, too," said Mom.

"I can help," said Matt.

"I'll help, too," said Rose.

4

"No, Rose," said Mom.
"You're too little to work
on a roof.
You can fix up your playhouse
today. Have some fun."

The Fixit family got to work.
Matt got the ladder.
Pop got some wood.
Mom got a hammer and
a bag of nails.

Nana gave Rose a hug.
"Cheer up, Rose," she said.
"You can help me
in the kitchen."
But Rose did not want
to cook.
She wanted to bang on nails
with a hammer.

The Fixit family worked and worked to fix the roof.

8

Rose worked, too.
She fixed the roof
on her playhouse.

11

The sky got dark.
"Hurry!" Mom said.
"I just felt a drop of rain."

Then the rain came down hard.
"The roof is leaking!" said Nana.
"It's raining in my kitchen!"

Mom, Pop, and Matt
came down the ladder.
They were very wet.

"Where is Rose?" Mom asked.

"There she is," said Nana.

"Come on in!" said Rose.
"My roof is not leaking."

15

The next day, the rain stopped.
The Fixit family fixed
their old roof.
And this time,
they let Rose help.